This book belongs to:

____

For Alyssia and Archer

First paperback edition Feb 2023

Book design by Yuliana Makhroyani

ISBN 978-1-7392828-0-6

The Only One In the World

Charlotte and Joe were busy building
the best castle in the world.

"Joe, do you think I'm the only one in the world holding a tiny yellow brick, just like this one right now?" asked Charlotte.

"Nope, I think there are 100 others," answered Joe, feeling smart.

"Do you think I'm the only one in the world to be chucking Joey this high right now?"

“Maybe. I bet I'm the only one in the world doing this right now,” Charlotte giggled, wiggling her bum and waving her hands all around.

“Then, I'm the only one in the world doing this.” Joe stuck his finger up his nose and poked out his tongue.

Spinning around the room and leaping into the air, Charlotte said,"I bet I'm the only one in the world dancing ballet in roller skates."

Joe stood tall with one arm stretched to the sky. "Well, I'm the only one in the world shooting to the moon in my supersonic rocket boots!"

"I'm the only one in the world who is breathing like a fish and swimming in the reef. Look! I can see a mermaid!"

"There's a black hole.
I'm the only one in the world jumping back to the time of the dinosaurs and riding on a flying dinosaur's back."

"I'm the only one in the world
surfing on a stingray."

"I'm the only one riding my quad bike
and chasing some ferocious lions
through the Amazon!"

"Watch out, Joe!" cried Charlotte.
"I'm the only one in the world to be
taming a fearsome dragon with my
mighty purple glitter sword."

Joe crouched down low and stuck out his arms. "I'm the only one in the world snowboarding down a glacier with polar bears and they're wearing sunglasses!"

"But Daaaaad, we're playing, The Only One in the World!"

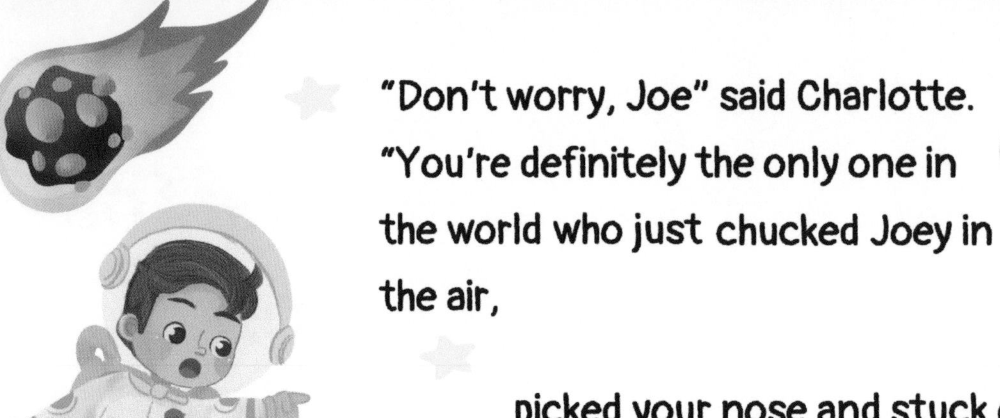

"Don't worry, Joe" said Charlotte.
"You're definitely the only one in
the world who just chucked Joey in
the air,

picked your nose and stuck out your tongue.

Shot up to the moon in your
supersonic rocket boots.

Flew on a dinosaurs back,
chased lions in the Amazon

Snowboarded down a glacier with polar bears
wearing sunglasses,

and has the hump about eating dinner."

"You're right,"said Joe, feeling much better.
"And you're the only one in the world who,
held a yellow brick,

wiggled your bum, waved your hands all around,

danced ballet in roller skates,

swam in the reef and saw the mermaids,

surfed on a sting ray,

tamed a fearsome dragon with your mighty
purple glitter sword,

All before having your dinner."

Just as they were about to eat, they heard
the familiar rattle of a key opening the front door.

Joe excitedly told Mum and Dad all about his day and the super fun day Charlotte started.
"You lot are the only ones in the world that I want to come home to," said Mum with a huge smile.

What are you doing right now?
Do you think you're the only one doing the exact same thing?

You could be the only one in the world reading this book, THIS VERY MOMENT and even if you are not....

THERE IS ONLY ONE
YOU
IN THE WORLD !!!

About the Author,

Kelly Miles is a firefighter and children's book author.

When she is not driving round in a big red fire truck, doing fire safety visits or fighting fires, she is creating new characters and thinking up fun, light-hearted stories full of excitement, imagination, friendship and charm.

She lives with her husband, 2 sons and moody cat Binksy. Kelly loves being outside and believes there is no better place to find inspiration. She is often seen going for long walks or runs through Epping Forest.

A little message from Kelly

Thank you for choosing this book. I hope you had as much fun reading it as I did writing it.

DID YOU SPOT Cybil the squirrel? Cybil likes to hide somewhere within the pages of my books. Well done if you found him. Don't forget to look out for him in the next one!

If you would like to colour in your own copy of The Only One in the World, pop over to:

https://mileskel.wixsite.com/kelly-miles
and download your free copy.
Be sure to share your amazing creations at:
kelly_miles_author
I can't wait to see them.
Much Love,
Kelly x

Printed in Great Britain
by Amazon